HORRID HENRY'S UNDERPANTS

Meet HORRID HENRY
the laugh-out-loud
worldwide sensation!

....

★ Over 15 million copies sold in 27
   countries and counting

★ # 1 chapter book series in the UK

★ Francesca Simon is the only American
   author to ever win the Galaxy British
   Book Awards Children's Book of the year
   (past winners include J.K. Rowling, Philip
   Pullman, and Eoin Colfer).

"Horrid Henry is a fabulous antihero…**a modern comic classic**." —*Guardian*

"**Wonderfully appealing to girls and boys alike**, a precious rarity at this age." —Judith Woods, *Times*

....

"The best children's comic writer."
                                        —Amanda Craig, *Times*

....

"**I love the Horrid Henry books by Francesca Simon**. They have lots of funny bits in. And Henry always gets into trouble!" —Mia, age 6, *BBC Learning Is Fun*

"My two boys love this book, and **I have actually had tears running down my face and had to stop reading because of laughing so hard**." —T. Franklin, Parent

"**It's easy to see why Horrid Henry is the bestselling character for five- to eight-year-olds**." —*Liverpool Echo*

"Francesca Simon's truly horrific little boy is **a monstrously enjoyable creation**. Parents love them because Henry makes their own little darlings seem like angels." —*Guardian Children's Books Supplement*

"I have tried out the Horrid Henry books with groups of children as a parent, as a babysitter, and as a teacher. **Children love to either hear them read aloud or to read them themselves**." —Danielle Hall, Teacher

"A flicker of recognition must pass through most teachers and parents when they read Horrid Henry. **There's a tiny bit of him in all of us.**" —Nancy Astee, *Child Education*

"**As a teacher...it's great to get a series of books my class loves.** They go mad for Horrid Henry." —A teacher

"**Henry is a beguiling hero who has entranced millions of reluctant readers.**" —*Herald*

....

"AN absolutely fantastic series and surely a winner with all children. Long live Francesca Simon and her brilliant books! More, more please!"   —A parent

....

"**Laugh-out-loud reading for both adults and children alike.**" —A parent

"**Horrid Henry certainly lives up to his name, and his antics are everything you hope your own child will avoid—which is precisely why younger children so enjoy these tales.**" —*Independent on Sunday*

"Henry might be unbelievably naughty, totally wicked, and utterly horrid, but **he is frequently credited with converting the most reluctant readers into enthusiastic ones**...superb in its simplicity." —*Liverpool Echo*

"Will make you laugh out loud."
—Sunday Times

"Parents reading them aloud may be consoled to discover that Henry can always be relied upon to behave worse than any of their own offspring." —*Independent*

"**What is brilliant about the books is that Henry never does anything that is subversive.** She creates an aura of supreme naughtiness (of which children are in awe) but points out that he operates within a safe and secure world... **eminently readable** books." —Emily Turner, *Angels and Urchins*

"Inventive and funny, with appeal for boys and girls alike, and super illustrations by Tony Ross." —Jewish Chronicle

"Accompanied by fantastic black-and-white drawings, the book is a joy to read. **Horrid Henry has an irresistible appeal to everyone—child and adult alike!** He is the child everyone is familiar with—irritating, annoying, but you still cannot help laughing when he gets into yet another scrape. Not quite a devil in disguise but you cannot help wondering at times! No wonder he is so popular!" —Angela Youngman

Horrid Henry by Francesca Simon

Horrid Henry

Horrid Henry Tricks the Tooth Fairy

Horrid Henry and the Mega-Mean Time Machine

Horrid Henry's Stinkbomb

Horrid Henry and the Mummy's Curse

Horrid Henry and the Soccer Fiend

Horrid Henry's Underpants

Horrid Henry and the Scary Sitter

Horrid Henry's Christmas

HORRID HENRY'S UNDERPANTS

Francesca Simon
Illustrated by Tony Ross

Jabberwocky SOURCEBOOKS
AN IMPRINT OF SOURCEBOOKS

Published by Sourcebooks Jabberwocky, an imprint of Sourcebooks, Inc.
P.O. Box 4410, Naperville, Illinois 60567-4410
(630) 961-3900
Fax: (630) 961-2168
www.sourcebooks.com

Originally published in Great Britain in 2003 by Orion Children's Books.

Library of Congress Cataloging-in-Publication Data

Simon, Francesca.
  Horrid Henry's underpants / Francesca Simon ; illustrated by Tony
Ross.
    p. cm.
  Originally published: Great Britain : Orion Children's Books, 2003.
  ISBN 978-1-4022-3825-3
  [1. Behavior—Fiction.] I. Ross, Tony, ill. II. Title.
  PZ7.S604Hsu 2009
  [Fic]—dc22
                          2008039691

            Printed and bound in the United States of America.
                          VP 10 9

Source of Product: Versa Press, Inc. East Peoria, IL, USA
Date of Production: April 2016
Run Number: 5006206

For Gina Kovarsky

CONTENTS

1

HORRID HENRY EATS A VEGETABLE

"Ugggh! Gross! Yuck! Bleccccch!"

Horrid Henry glared at the horrible, disgusting food slithering on his plate. Globby slobby blobs. Bumpy lumps. Rubbery blubbery globules of glop. Ugghh!

How Dad and Mom and Peter could eat this swill without throwing up was amazing. Henry poked at the white, knobbly clump. It looked like brains. It felt like brains. Maybe it was... Ewwwwwwww.

Horrid Henry pushed away his plate.

"I can't eat this," moaned Henry. "I'll be sick!"

"Henry! Cauliflower cheese is delicious," said Mom.

"And nutritious," said Dad.

"I love it," said Perfect Peter. "Can I have seconds?"

"It's nice to know *someone* appreciates my cooking," said Dad. He frowned at Henry.

"But I hate vegetables," said Henry. Yuck. Vegetables were so... healthy. And tasted so... vegetably. "I want pizza!"

"Well, you can't have it," said Dad.

"Ralph has pizza and fries every night at *his* house," said Henry. "And Graham *never* has to eat vegetables."

"I don't care what Ralph and Graham eat," said Mom.

"You've got to eat more vegetables," said Dad.

"I eat lots of vegetables," said Henry.

"Name one," said Dad.

"Chips," said Henry.

"Chips aren't vegetables, are they, Mom?" said Perfect Peter.

"No," said Mom. "Go on, Henry."

"Ketchup," said Henry.

"Ketchup is not a vegetable," said Dad.

"It's impossible cooking for you," said Mom.

"You're such a picky eater," said Dad.

"I eat lots of things," said Henry.

"Like what?" said Dad.

"Fries. Chips. Burgers. Pizza. Chocolate. Candy. Cake. Cookies. Lots of food," said Horrid Henry.

"That's not very healthy, Henry," said Perfect Peter. "You haven't said any fruit or vegetables."

"So?" said Henry. "Mind your own business, Toad."

"Henry called me Toad," wailed Peter.

"Ribbet. Ribbet," croaked Horrid Henry.

"Don't be horrid, Henry," snapped Dad.

"You can't go on eating so unhealthily," said Mom.

"Agreed," said Dad.

Uh oh, thought Henry. Here it comes. Nag nag nag. If there were prizes for best naggers, Mom and Dad would win every time.

"I'll make a deal with you, Henry," said Mom.

"What?" said Henry suspiciously. Mom and Dad's "deals" usually involved his doing something horrible, for a pathetic reward. Well no way was he falling for that again.

"If you eat all your vegetables for five nights in a row, we'll take you to Gobble and Go."

Henry's heart missed a beat. Gobble and Go! Gobble and Go! Only Henry's favorite restaurant in the whole wide world. Their motto: "The fries just keep on coming!" shone forth from a purple neon sign. Music blared from twenty loudspeakers. Each table had its own TV. You could watch the chefs heat up your food in a giant microwave. Best of all, grown-ups never wanted to hang around for hours and chat. You ordered, gobbled, and left. Heaven.

And what fantastic food! Jumbo burgers. Huge pizzas. Lakes of ketchup. As many fries as you could eat. Fifty-two different ice creams. And not a vegetable in sight.

For some reason Mom and Dad hated Gobble and Go. They'd taken him once, and sworn they would never go again.

And now, unbelievably, Mom was offering.

"Deal!" shouted Henry, in case she changed her mind.

"So we're agreed," said Mom. "You eat your vegetables every night for five nights, and then we'll go."

"Sure. Whatever," said Horrid Henry eagerly. He'd agree to anything for a meal at Gobble and Go. He'd agree to dance naked down the street singing "Hallelujah! I'm a nudie!" for the chance to eat at Gobble and Go.

Perfect Peter stopped eating his cauliflower. He didn't look very happy.

"I always eat *my* vegetables," said Peter. "What's my reward?"

"Health," said Mom.

Day 1. String beans.

"Mom, Henry hasn't eaten any beans yet," said Peter.

"I have too," lied Henry.

"No you haven't," said Peter. "I've been watching."

"Shut up, Peter," said Henry.

"Mom!" wailed Peter. "Henry told me to shut up."

"Don't tell your brother to shut up," said Mom.

"It's rude," said Dad. "Now eat your veggies."

Horrid Henry glared at his plate, teeming with slimy string beans. Just like a bunch of green worms, he thought. Yuck.

He must
have been crazy
agreeing to eat
vegetables for five
nights in a row.
He'd be poisoned
before day three.

Then they'd be
sorry. "How could we have been so
cruel?" Mom would shriek. "We've
killed our own son," Dad would moan.
"Why oh why did we make him eat his
greens?" they would sob.

Too bad he'd be dead so he couldn't
scream, "I told you so!"

"We have a deal, Henry," said Dad.

"I know," snapped Henry.

He cut off the teeniest, tiniest bit of
string bean he could.

"Go on," said Mom.

Slowly, Horrid Henry lifted his fork
and put the poison in his mouth.

Aaaarrrgggghhhhhh! What a horrible

taste! Henry spat and spluttered as the sickening sliver of string bean stuck in his throat.

"Water!" he gasped.

Perfect Peter speared several beans and popped them in his mouth.

"Great string beans, Dad," said Peter. "So crispy and crunchy."

"Have mine if you like them so much," muttered Henry.

"I want to see you eat every one of those string beans," said Dad. "Or no Gobble and Go."

Horrid Henry scowled. No way was he eating another mouthful. The taste was too horrible. But, oh, Gobble and Go. Those burgers! Those fries! Those TVs!

There had to be another way. Surely he, King Henry the Horrible, could defeat a plate of greens?

Horrid Henry worked out his battle

plan. It was dangerous. It was risky. But what choice did he have?

First, he had to distract the enemy.

"You know, Mom," said Henry, pretending to chew, "you were right. These beans *are* very tasty."

Mom beamed.

Dad beamed.

"I told you you'd like them if you tried them," said Mom.

Henry pretended to swallow, then speared another bean. He pushed it around his plate.

Mom got up to refill the water jug. Dad turned to speak to her. Now was his chance!

Horrid Henry stretched out his foot under the table and lightly tickled Peter's leg.

"Look out, Peter, there's a spider on your leg."

"Where?" squealed Peter, looking frantically under the table.

Leap! Plop!

Henry's beans hopped onto Peter's plate.

Peter raised his head.

"I don't see any spider," said Peter.

"I knocked it off," mumbled Henry, pretending to chew vigorously.

Then Peter saw his plate, piled high with string beans.

"Ooh," said Peter, "lucky me! I thought I'd finished!"

Tee hee, thought Horrid Henry.

Day 2. Broccoli.

Plip!

A piece of Henry's broccoli "accidentally" fell on the floor. Henry kicked it under Peter's chair.

Plop! Another piece of Henry's broccoli fell. And another. And another.

Plip plop. Plip plop. Plip plop.

Soon the floor under Peter's chair was littered with broccoli bits.

"Mom!" said Henry. "Peter's making a mess."

"Don't be a tattletale, Henry," said Dad.

"He's always telling on *me*," said Henry.

Dad checked under Peter's chair.

"Peter! Eat more carefully. You're not a baby any more."

Ha ha ha, thought Horrid Henry.

Day 3. Peas.

Squish!

Henry flattened a pea under his knife. Squash!

Henry flattened another one.

Squish. Squash.

Squish. Squash.

Soon every pea was safely squished and hidden under Henry's knife.

"Great dinner, Dad," said Horrid Henry. "Especially the peas. I'll clear," he added, carrying his plate to the sink and quickly rinsing his knife.

Dad beamed.

"Eating vegetables is making you helpful," said Dad.

"Yes," said Henry sweetly. "It's great being helpful."

Day 4. Cabbage.

Buzz.

Buzz.

"A fly landed on my cabbage!" shrieked Henry. He swatted the air with his hands.

"Where?" said Mom.

"There!" said Henry. He leapt out of his seat. "Now it's on the fridge!"

"Buzz," said Henry under his breath.

"I don't see any fly," said Dad.

"Up there!" said Henry, pointing to the ceiling.

Mom looked up.

Dad looked up.

Peter looked up.

Henry dumped a handful of cabbage in the garbage. Then he sat back down at the table.

"Rats," said Henry. "I can't eat the rest of my cabbage now, can I? Not after a filthy, horrible, disgusting fly has walked all over it, spreading germs and dirt and poo and—"

"All right, all right," said Dad. "Leave the rest."

I am a genius, thought Horrid Henry, smirking. Only one more battle until—Vegetable Victory!

★ ★ ★

16

Day 5. Sprouts.

Mom ate her sprouts.

Dad ate his sprouts.

Peter ate his sprouts.

Henry glared at his sprouts. Of all the miserable, rotten vegetables ever invented, sprouts were the worst. So bitter. So stomach-churning. So...green.

But how to get rid of them? There was Peter's head, a tempting target. A very tempting target. Henry's sprout-flicking fingers itched. No, thought Horrid Henry. I can't blow it when I'm so close.

Should he throw them on the floor? Spit them in his napkin?

Or—Horrid Henry beamed.

There was a little drawer in the table in front of Henry's chair. A perfect, brussels sprout-sized drawer.

Henry eased it open. What could be simpler than stuffing a sprout or two inside while pretending to eat?

Soon the drawer was full. Henry's plate was empty.

"Look Mom! Look Dad!" screeched Henry. "All gone!" Which was true, he thought gleefully.

"Good job, Henry," said Dad.

"Good job, Henry," said Peter.

"We'll take you to Gobble and Go tomorrow," said Mom.

"Yippee!" screamed Horrid Henry.

Mom, Dad, Henry, and Peter walked up the street.

Mom, Dad, Henry, and Peter walked down the street.

Where was Gobble and Go, with its flashing neon sign, blaring music, and purple walls? They must have walked past it.

But how? Horrid Henry looked around wildly. It was impossible to miss Gobble and Go. You could see that neon sign for miles.

"It was right here," said Horrid
Henry.

But Gobble and Go was gone.

A new restaurant squatted in its place.

"The Virtuous Veggie," read the sign.
"The all new vegetable restaurant!"

Horrid Henry gazed in horror at the
menu posted outside.

> Cabbage Casserole
> Pop-up Peas
> Spinach Surprise
> Sprouts a go-go
> Choice of rhubarb or
> broccoli ice cream

"Yummy!" said Perfect Peter.

"Look, Henry," said Mom. "It's
serving all your new favorite vegetables."

Horrid Henry opened his mouth to
protest. Then he closed it. He knew
when he was beaten.

2

....

HORRID HENRY'S UNDERPANTS

A late birthday present! Whoopee! Just when you thought you'd got all your loot, more treasure arrives.

Horrid Henry shook the small thin package. It was light. Very light. Maybe it was—oh, please let it be—MONEY! Of course it was money. What else could it be? There was so much stuff he needed: a Mutant Max lunchbox, a Rapper Zapper Blaster, and, of course, the new Terminator Gladiator game he kept seeing advertised on TV. Mom and Dad were so mean and horrible, they wouldn't buy it for him. But he could buy whatever he liked with his own money.

So there. Ha ha ha ha ha. Wouldn't Ralph be green with envy when he swaggered into school with a Mutant Max lunchbox? And no way would he even let Peter touch his Rapper Zapper Blaster.

So how much money had he been sent? Maybe enough for him to buy everything! Horrid Henry tore off the wrapping paper.

AAAAARRRRGGGHHHHH! Great-Aunt Greta had done it again.

Great-Aunt Greta thought he was a girl. Great-Aunt Greta had been told ten billion times that his name was Henry, not Henrietta, and that he wasn't four years old. But every year Peter would get $10, or a football, or a computer game, and he would get a Walkie-Talkie-Teasy-Weasy-Burpy-Slurpy Doll. Or a Princess Pamper Parlor. Or Baby Poopie Pants. And now this.

Horrid Henry picked up the birthday

card. Maybe there was money inside.
He opened it.

> *Dear Henny,*
> *You must be such a big girl now, so I know*
> *you'd love a pair of big girl underpants. I'll bet*
> *pink is your favorite color.*
> *Love, Great-Aunt Greta*

Horrid Henry stared in horror at the
frilly pink lacy underpants, decorated
with glittery hearts and bows. This
was the worst present he had ever
received. Worse than socks. Worse than
handkerchiefs. Even worse than a book.
　　Bleccch! Ick! Yuck!
Horrid Henry
chucked the
hideous underpants
in the garbage
where they
belonged.

Ding dong.

Oh no! Rude Ralph was here to play. If he saw those underpants Henry would never hear the end of it. His name would be mud forever.

Clump clump clump.

Ralph was stomping up the stairs to his bedroom. Henry snatched the terrible underpants from the garbage and looked around his room wildly for a hiding place. Under the pillow? What if they had a pillow fight? Under the bed? What if they played hide and seek? Quickly Henry stuffed them in the back of his underpants drawer. I'll get rid of them the moment Ralph leaves, he thought.

"Mercy, Your Majesty, mercy!" King Henry the Horrible looked down at his sniveling brother.

"Off with his head!" he ordered.

"Henry! Henry! Henry!" cheered his grateful subjects.

"HENRY!"

King Henry the Horrible woke up. His Medusa mother was looming above him.

"You've overslept!" shrieked Mom. "School starts in five minutes! Get dressed! Quick! Quick!" She pulled the blanket off Henry.

"Wha—wha?" mumbled Henry.

Dad raced into the room.

"Hurry!" shouted Dad. "We're late!" He yanked Henry out of bed.

Henry stumbled around his dark bedroom. Half-asleep, he reached inside his underwear drawer, grabbed a pair, then picked up some clothes off the floor and flung everything on. Then he, Dad, and Peter ran all the way to school.

"Margaret! Stop pulling Susan's hair!"

"Ralph! Sit down!"

"Linda! Sit up!"

"Henry! Pay attention!" barked Miss Battle-Axe. "I am about to explain long division. I will only explain it once. You take a great big number, like 374, and then divide it—"

Horrid Henry was not paying attention. He was tired. He was crabby. And for some reason his underpants were itchy.

These underpants feel horrible, he thought. And so tight. What's wrong with them?

Horrid Henry sneaked a peek.

And then
Horrid Henry saw
what underpants he
had on. Not
his Driller Cannibal
underpants. Not his
Marvin the Maniac
ones either. Not
even his old Gross-
Out ones, with the
holes and the droopy elastic.

He, Horrid Henry, was wearing frilly
pink lacy girls' underpants covered in
glittery hearts and bows. He'd completely
forgotten he'd stuffed them into his
underpants drawer last month so Ralph
wouldn't see them. And now, oh horror
of horrors, he was wearing them.

Maybe it's a nightmare, thought
Horrid Henry hopefully. He pinched
his arm. Ouch! Then, just to be sure, he
pinched William.

"Waaaaah!" wailed Weepy William.

"Stop weeping, William!" said Miss
Battle-Axe. "Now, what number do I
need—"

It was not a nightmare. He was still in
school, still wearing pink underpants.

What to do, what to do?

Don't panic, thought Horrid Henry.
He took a deep breath. Don't panic.
After all, no one will know. His pants
weren't see-through or anything.

Wait. What pants was he wearing?
Were there any holes in them? Quickly
Horrid Henry twisted round to check his
bottom.

Phew. There were no holes. What
luck he hadn't put on his old jeans with
the big rip but a new pair.

He was safe.

"Henry! What's the answer?" said
Miss Battle-Axe.

"Pants," said Horrid Henry before he
could stop himself.

The class burst out laughing.

"Pants!" screeched Rude Ralph.

"Pants!" screeched Dizzy Dave.

"Henry. Stand up," ordered Miss
Battle-Axe.

Henry stood. His heart was
pounding.

Slip!

Aaaarrrghhh! The lacy ruffle of his
pink underpants was showing! His
new pants were too big. Mom always
bought him clothes that were way too
big so he'd grow into them. These were
the falling-down ones he'd tried on
yesterday. Henry gripped his pants tight
and yanked them up.

"What did you say?" said Miss Battle-Axe slowly.

"Ants," said Horrid Henry.

"Ants?" said Miss Battle-Axe.

"Yeah," said Henry quickly. "I was just thinking about how many ants you could divide by—by that number you said," he added.

Miss Battle-Axe glared at him.

"I've got my eye on you, Henry," she snapped. "Now sit down and pay attention."

Henry sat. All he had to do was tuck in his T-shirt. That would keep his pants up. He'd look stupid but for once Henry didn't care.

Just so long as no one ever knew about his pink lacy underpants.

And then Henry's blood turned to ice. What was the latest craze on the playground? Depantsing. Who'd started it? Horrid Henry. Yesterday he'd chased Dizzy

Dave and pulled down his pants. The day
before he'd done the same thing to Rude
Ralph. Just this morning he'd depantsed
Tough Toby on the way into class.

They'd all be trying to depants him
now.

I have to get another pair of
underpants, thought Henry desperately.

Miss Battle-Axe passed around the
math worksheets. Quickly Horrid Henry
scribbled down: 3, 7, 41, 174, without
reading any questions. He didn't have
time for long division.

Where could he find some other
underpants? He could pretend to be sick
and get sent home from school. But
he'd already tried that twice this week.
Wait. Wait. He was brilliant. He was a
genius. What about the Lost and Found?
Someone, some time, must have lost some
underpants.

DING! DING!

Before the playtime bell had finished
ringing Horrid Henry was out of his
seat and racing down the hall, holding
tight to his pants. He checked carefully
to make sure no one was watching, then
ducked into the Lost and Found. He'd
hide here until he found some underpants.

The Lost and Found was stuffed with
clothes. He rummaged through the
mountains of lost shoes, socks, jackets,
pants, shirts, coats, lunchboxes, hats,
and gloves. I'm amazed anyone leaves
school wearing *anything*, thought Horrid

32

Henry, tossing another sweatshirt over his shoulder.

Then—hurray! Underpants. A pair of blue underpants. What a wonderful sight.

Horrid Henry pulled the underpants from the pile. Oh no. They were the teeniest, tiniest pair he'd ever seen. Some toddler must have lost them.

Rats, thought Horrid Henry. Well, no way was he wearing his horrible pink underpants a second longer. He'd just have to trade underpants with someone. And Horrid Henry had the perfect someone in mind.

Henry found Peter in the playground playing tag with Tidy Ted.

"I need to talk to you in private," said Henry. "It's urgent."

"What about?" said Peter cautiously.

"It's top secret," said Henry. Out of the corner of his eye he saw Dave and Toby sneaking toward him.

Top secret! Henry never shared top secret secrets with Peter.

"Quick!" yelped Henry. "There's no time to lose!"

He ducked into the boys' bathroom. Peter followed.

"Peter, I'm worried about you," said Horrid Henry. He tried to look concerned.

"I'm fine," said Peter.

"No you're not," said Henry. "I've heard bad things about you."

"What bad things?" said Peter anxiously. Not—not that he had run across the carpet in class?

"Embarrassing rumors," said Horrid
Henry. "But if I don't tell you, who
will? After all," he said, putting his arm
around Peter's shoulder, "it's my job to
look after you. Big brothers should look
out for little ones."

Perfect Peter could not believe his
ears.

"Oh, Henry," said Peter. "I've always
wanted a brother who looked out for me."

"That's me," said Henry. "Now listen.
I've heard you wear baby underpants."

"I do not," said Peter. "Look!" And

he showed Henry his Daffy and her
Dancing Daisies underpants.

Horrid Henry's heart went cold.
Daffy and her Dancing Daisies! Ugh.
Yuck. Gross. But even Daffy would be
a million billion times better than pink
underpants with lace ruffles.

"Daffy Daisy are the most babyish
underpants you could wear," said Henry.
"Worse than wearing a diaper. Everyone
will tease you."

Peter's lip trembled. He hated being
teased.

"What can I do?" he asked.

Henry pretended to think. "Look.
I'll do you a big favor. I'll swap my
underpants for yours. That way *I'll* get
teased, not you."

"Thank you, Henry," said Peter.
"You're the best brother in the world."
Then he stopped.

"Wait a minute," he said suspiciously,
"let's see your underpants."

"Why?" said Henry.

"Because," said Peter, "how do I know you've even got underpants to swap?"

Horrid Henry was outraged.

"Of course I've got underpants," said Henry.

"Then show me," said Peter.

Horrid Henry was trapped.

"OK," he said, giving Peter a quick flash of pink lace.

Perfect Peter stared at Henry's underpants.

"Those are your underpants?" he said.

"Sure," said Horrid Henry. "These are big boy underpants."

"But they're pink," said Peter.

"All big boys wear pink," said Henry.

"But they have lace on them," said Peter.

"All big boys' pants have lace," said Henry.

"But they have hearts and bows," said Peter.

"Of course they do, they're big boy underpants," said Horrid Henry. "You wouldn't know because you only wear baby underpants."

Peter hesitated.

"But...but...they look like—girls' underpants," said Peter.

Henry snorted. "Girls' underpants! Do you think *I'd* ever wear girls' underpants? These are what all the big kids are wearing. You'll be the coolest kid in class in these."

Perfect Peter backed away.

"No I won't," said Peter.

"Yes you will," said Henry.

"I don't want to wear your smelly underpants," said Peter.

"They're not smelly," said Henry. "They're brand new. Now give me your underpants."

"NO!" screamed Peter.

"YES!" screamed Henry. "Give me your underpants!"

"What's going on in here?" came a voice of steel. It was the principal, Mrs. Oddbod.

"Nothing," said Henry.

"There's no hanging around the bathroom at playtime," said Mrs. Oddbod. "Out of here, both of you."

Peter ran out the door.

Now what do I do, thought Horrid Henry.

Henry ducked into a stall and hid the pink underpants on the ledge above the third toilet. No way was he putting those underpants back on. Better Henry No Underpants than Henry Pink Underpants.

★ ★ ★

At lunchtime Horrid Henry dodged
Graham. He dodged Toby by the
climbing frame. During last play Dave
almost caught him by the water
fountain but Henry was too quick.
Ralph chased him into class but Henry
got to his seat just in time. He'd done
it! Only forty-five minutes to go until
home time. There'd be no depantsing
after school with parents around.
Henry couldn't believe it. He was safe
at last.

He stuck out his tongue at Ralph.

"Nah nah ne nah ne," he jeered.

Miss Battle-Axe clapped her claws.

"Time to change for P.E." said Miss
Battle-Axe.

P.E.! It couldn't be—not a P.E. day.

"And I don't care if aliens stole your
P.E. uniform, Henry," said Miss Battle-
Axe, glaring at him. "No excuses."

That's what she thought. He had the

perfect excuse. Even a teacher as mean
and horrible as Miss Battle-Axe would not
force a boy to do P.E. without underpants.

Horrid Henry went up to Miss Battle-
Axe and whispered in her ear.

"Forgot your underpants, eh?" barked
Miss Battle-Axe loudly.

Henry
blushed scarlet.
When he
was king he'd
make Miss
Battle-Axe
walk around
town every
day wearing underpants on her head.

"Well, Henry, today is your lucky
day," said Miss Battle-Axe, pulling
something pink and lacy out of her
pocket. "I found these in the boys'
bathroom."

"Take them away!" screamed Horrid
Henry.

3

HORRID HENRY'S SICK DAY

Cough! Cough!

Sneeze! Sneeze!

"Are you all right, Peter?" asked Mom.

Peter coughed, choked, and spluttered.

"I'm OK," he gasped.

"Are you sure?" said Dad. "You don't look very well."

"It's nothing," said Perfect Peter, coughing.

Mom felt Peter's sweaty brow.

"You've got a temperature," said Mom. "I think you'd better stay home from school today."

"But I don't want to miss school," said Peter.

"Go back to bed,"
said Mom.

"But I want to go
to school," wailed
Peter. "I'm sure I'll
be—" Peter's pale,
sweaty face turned
green. He dashed up the

stairs to the bathroom. Mom ran after him.

Blecccccccchhhh. The horrible sound
of vomiting filled the house.

Horrid Henry stopped eating his toast.
Peter, stay at home? Peter, miss school?
Peter, lying around watching TV while he,
Henry, had to suffer a long hard day with
Miss Battle-Axe?
No way!
He was sick,
too. Hadn't he
coughed twice
this morning?
And he had
definitely sneezed

last night. Now that he thought about it, he could feel those flu germs invading. Yup, there they were, marching down his throat.

Stomp, stomp, stomp marched the germs. Mercy! shrieked his throat. Ha ha ha gloated the germs.

Horrid Henry thought about those spelling words he hadn't learned. The map he hadn't finished coloring. The book report he hadn't done.

Oww. His throat hurt.

Oooh. His tummy hurt.

Eeek. His head hurt.

Yippee! He was sick!

So what would it be?

Math or Mutant Max?

Reading or relaxing?

Commas or comics?

Tests or TV?

Hmmm, thought Horrid Henry. Hard choice.

Cough. Cough.

45

Dad continued reading the paper.

COUGH! COUGH! COUGH!
COUGH! COUGH!

"Are you all right, Henry?" asked
Dad, without looking up.

"No!" gasped Henry. "I'm sick, too. I
can't go to school."

Slowly Dad put down his newspaper.

"You don't look ill, Henry," said Dad.

"But I am," whimpered Horrid Henry.
He clutched his throat. "My throat really
hurts," he moaned. Then he added a few
coughs, just in case.

"I feel weak," he groaned.
"Everything aches."

Dad sighed.

"All right, you can stay home," he said.

Yes! thought Horrid Henry. He was
amazed. It usually took much more
moaning and groaning before his mean,
horrible parents decided he was sick
enough to miss a day of school.

"But no playing on the computer," said Dad. "If you're sick, you have to lie down."

Horrid Henry was outraged.

"But it makes me feel better to play on the computer," he protested.

"If you're well enough to play on the computer, you're well enough to go to school," said Dad.

Rats.

Oh well, thought Horrid Henry. He'd get his blanket, lie on the sofa and watch lots of TV instead. Then Mom would

bring him cold drinks, lunch on a tray, maybe even ice cream. It was always such a waste when you were too sick to enjoy being sick, thought Horrid Henry happily.

He could hear Mom and Dad arguing upstairs.

"I need to go to work," said Mom.

"I need to go to work," said Dad.

"I stayed home last time," said Mom.

"No you didn't, I did," said Dad.

"Are you sure?" said Mom.

"Yes," said Dad.

"Are you sure you're sure?" said Mom.

Horrid Henry could hardly believe his ears. Imagine arguing over who got to stay home! When he was grown-up he was going to stay home full time, testing computer games for a million dollars a week.

He bounced into the sitting room. Then he stopped bouncing. A horrible, ugly, snotty creature was stretched out

under a blanket in the comfy black chair.
Horrid Henry glanced at the TV.
A dreadful assortment of wobbling
creatures were dancing and prancing.

TRA LA LA LA LA,
WE LIVE AT NELLIE'S
WE'VE ALL GOT BIG BELLIES
WE EAT PURPLE JELLIES
AT NELLIE'S NURSERY (tee hee)

Horrid Henry sat down on the sofa.

"I want to watch *Robot Rebels*," said
Henry.

"I'm watching *Nellie's Nursery*," said
Peter, sniffing.

"Stop sniffing," said Henry.

"I can't help it, my nose is running,"
said Peter.

"I'm sicker than you, and *I'm* not
sniffing," said Henry.

"I'm sicker than you," said Peter.

"Faker."

"Faker."

"Liar."

"Liar!"

"MOM!" shrieked Henry and Peter.

Mom came into the room, carrying a tray of cold drinks and two thermometers.

"Henry's being mean to me!" whined Peter.

"Peter's being mean to *me!*" whined Henry.

"If you're well enough to fight, you're well enough to go to school, Henry," said Mom, glaring at him.

"I wasn't fighting, Peter was," said Henry.

"Henry was," said Peter, coughing.

Henry coughed louder.

Peter groaned.

Henry groaned louder.

"Uggghhhhh," moaned Peter.

"Uggghhhhhhhhhh," moaned Henry.

"It's not fair. I want to watch *Robot Rebels*."

"I want to watch *Nellie's Nursery*," whimpered Peter.

"Peter will choose what to watch because he's the sickest," said Mom.

Peter, sicker than he was? As if. Well, no way was Henry's sick day going to be ruined by his horrible brother.

"I'm the sickest, Mom," protested Henry. "I just don't complain so much."

Mom looked tired. She popped one thermometer into Henry's mouth and the other into Peter's.

51

"I'll be back in five minutes to check them," she said. "And I don't want to hear another peep from either of you," she added, leaving the room.

Horrid Henry lay back weakly on the sofa with the thermometer in his mouth. He felt terrible. He touched his forehead. He was burning! His temperature must be 105!

I bet my temperature is so high the thermometer won't even have enough numbers, thought Henry. Just wait till Mom saw how ill he was. Then she'd be sorry she'd been so mean.

Perfect Peter started groaning. "I'm going to be sick," he gasped, taking the thermometer from his mouth and running from the room.

The moment Peter left, Henry leapt up from the sofa and checked Peter's thermometer. 101 degrees! Oh no, Peter had a temperature. Now Peter would

start getting *all* the attention. Mom
would make Henry fetch and carry for
him. Peter might even get extra ice
cream.

Something had to be
done.

Quickly Henry plunged
Peter's thermometer into
the glass of iced water.

Beep. Beep. Horrid
Henry took out his own
thermometer. It read 98.6
degrees. Normal.

Normal! His temperature was normal?
That was impossible. How could his
temperature be normal when he was
so ill?

If Mom saw that normal
temperature she'd have him
dressed for school in three
seconds. Obviously there
was something wrong with
that stupid thermometer.

53

Horrid Henry held it to the light
bulb. Just to warm it up a little, he
thought.

Clump. Clump.

Yikes! Mom was coming back.

Quickly Henry yanked Peter's
thermometer out of the iced water and
replaced his own in his mouth. Oww! It
was hot.

"Let's see if you have a temperature,"
said Mom. She took the thermometer
out of Henry's mouth.

"127 degrees!" she shrieked.

Oops.

"The thermometer must be broken,"
mumbled Henry. "But I still have a
temperature. I'm boiling."

"Hmm," said Mom, feeling Henry's
forehead.

Peter came back into the sitting room
slowly. His face was ashen.

"Check *my* temperature, Mom," said

Peter. He lay back weakly on the pillows.

Mom checked Peter's thermometer.

"57 degrees!" she shrieked.

Oops, thought Horrid Henry.

"That one must be broken too," said Henry.

He decided to change the subject fast.

"Mom, could you open the curtains please?" said Henry.

"But I want them closed," said Peter.

"Open!"

"Closed!"

"We'll leave them closed," said Mom.

Peter sneezed.

"Mom!" wailed Henry. "Peter got snot all over me."

"Mom!" wailed Peter. "Henry's smelly."

Horrid Henry glared at Peter.

Perfect Peter glared at Henry.

Henry whistled.

Peter hummed.

"Henry's whistling!"

"Peter's humming!"

"MOM!" they screamed. "Make him stop!"

"That's enough!" shouted Mom. "Go to your bedrooms, both of you!"

Henry and Peter heaved their heavy bones upstairs to their rooms.

"It's all your fault," said Henry.

"It's yours," said Peter.

The front door opened. Dad came in. He looked pale.

"I'm not feeling well," said Dad. "I'm going to bed."

Horrid Henry was bored. Horrid Henry was fed up. What was the point of being sick if you couldn't watch TV and you couldn't play on the computer?

"I'm hungry!" complained Horrid Henry.

"I'm thirsty," complained Perfect Peter.

"I'm achy," complained Dad.

"My bed's too hot!" moaned Horrid Henry.

"My bed's too cold," moaned Perfect Peter.

"My bed's too hot and too cold," moaned Dad.

Mom ran up the stairs.

Mom ran down the stairs.

"Ice cream!" shouted Horrid Henry.

"Hot water bottle!" shouted Perfect Peter.

"More pillows!" shouted Dad.

Mom walked up the stairs.

Mom walked down the stairs.

"Toast!" shouted Henry.

"Tissues!" croaked Peter.

"Tea!" gasped Dad.

"Can you wait a minute?" said Mom. "I need to sit down."

"NO!" shouted Henry, Peter, and Dad.

"All right," said Mom.

She plodded up the stairs.

She plodded down the stairs.

"My head is hurting!"

"My throat is hurting!"

"My stomach is hurting!"

Mom trudged up the stairs.

Mom trudged down the stairs.

"Chips," screeched Henry.

"Throat lozenge," croaked Peter.

"Tissue," wheezed Dad.

Mom staggered up the stairs.

Mom staggered down the stairs.

Then Horrid Henry saw the time. Three thirty. School was finished! The weekend was here! It was amazing, thought Horrid Henry, how much better he suddenly felt.

Horrid Henry threw off his blanket and leapt out of bed.

"Mom!" he shouted. "I'm feeling much better. Can I go and play on the computer now?"

Mom staggered into his room.

"Thank goodness you're better, Henry," she whispered. "I feel terrible. I'm going to bed. Could you bring me a cup of tea?"

What?

"I'm busy," snapped Henry.

Mom glared at him.

"All right," said Henry, grudgingly. Why couldn't Mom get her own tea? She had legs, didn't she?

Horrid Henry escaped into the living room. He sat down at the computer and loaded "Intergalactic Robot Rebellion: This Time It's Personal." Bliss. He'd zap some robots, then have a go at "Snake Master's Revenge."

"Henry!" gasped Mom. "Where's my tea?"

"Henry!" rasped Dad. "Bring me a drink of water!"

"Henry!" whimpered Peter. "Bring me an extra blanket."

60

Horrid Henry scowled. Honestly, how was he meant to concentrate with all these interruptions?

"Tea!"

"Water!"

"Blanket!"

"Get it yourself!" he howled. What was he, a servant?

"Henry!" spluttered Dad. "Come up here this minute."

Slowly, Horrid Henry got to his feet. He looked longingly at the flashing screen. But what choice did he have?

"I'm sick too!" shrieked Horrid Henry. "I'm going back to bed."

4

HORRID HENRY'S
THANK YOU LETTER

Ahh! This was the life! A sofa, a TV, a bag
of chips. Horrid Henry sighed happily.

"Henry!" shouted Mom from the
kitchen. "Are you watching TV?"

Henry blocked his ears. Nothing was
going to interrupt his new favorite TV
show, *Terminator Gladiator.*

"Answer me, Henry!" shouted Mom.
"Have you written your Christmas thank
you letters?"

"NO!" bellowed Henry.

"Why not?" screamed Mom.

"Because I haven't," said Henry. "I'm
busy." Couldn't she leave him alone for
two seconds?

Mom marched into the room and switched off the TV.

"Hey!" said Henry. "I'm watching *Terminator Gladiator.*"

"Too bad," said Mom. "I told you, no TV until you've written your thank you letters."

"It's not fair!" wailed Henry.

"I've written all *my* thank you letters," said Perfect Peter.

"Good job, Peter," said Mom. "Thank goodness *one* of my children has good manners."

Peter smiled modestly. "I always write mine the moment I unwrap a present. I'm a good boy, aren't I?"

"The best," said Mom.

"Oh, shut up, Peter," snarled Henry.

"Mom! Henry told me to shut up!" said Peter.

"Stop being horrid, Henry. You will

write to Aunt Ruby, Great-Aunt Greta
and Grandma now."

"Now?" moaned Henry. "Can't I do
it later?"

"When's later?" said Dad.

"Later!" said Henry. Why wouldn't
they stop nagging him about those
stupid letters?

Horrid Henry hated writing thank
you letters. Why should he waste his
precious time saying thank you for
presents? Time he could be spending
reading comics or watching TV. But
no. He would barely unwrap a present
before Mom started nagging. She even
expected him to write to Great-Aunt
Greta and thank her for the Baby
Poopie Pants doll. Great Aunt-Greta
for one did not deserve a thank you
letter.

This year Aunt Ruby had sent
him a hideous lime-green cardigan.

Why should he thank her for that? True,
Grandma had given him $15, which was
great. But then Mom had to spoil it by
making him write her a letter too. Henry
hated writing letters for nice presents
every bit as much as he hated writing
them for horrible ones.

"You have to write thank you letters,"
said Dad.

"But why?" said Henry.

"Because it's polite," said Dad.

"Because people have spent time and
money on you," said Mom.

So what? thought Horrid Henry.
Grown-ups had loads of time to do

whatever they wanted. No one told them,
stop watching TV and write a thank you
letter. Oh no. They could do it whenever
they felt like it. Or not even do it at all.

And adults had tons of money
compared to him. Why shouldn't they
spend it buying him presents?

"All you have to do is write one
page," said Dad. "What's the big deal?"

Henry stared at him. Did Dad have no
idea how long it would take him to write
one whole page? Hours and hours and
hours.

"You're the meanest, most horrible
parents in the world and I hate you!"
shrieked Horrid Henry.

"Go to your room, Henry!" shouted
Dad.

"And don't come down until you've
written those letters," shouted Mom. "I
am sick and tired of arguing about this."

Horrid Henry stomped upstairs.

Well, no way was he writing any thank
you letters. He'd rather starve. He'd rather
die. He'd stay in his room for a month. A
year. One day Mom and Dad would come
up to check on him and all they'd find
would be a few bones. Then they'd be sorry.

Actually, knowing them, they'd probably
just moan about the mess. And then Peter
would be all happy because he'd get Henry's
room and Henry's room was bigger.

Well, no way would he give them
the satisfaction. All right, thought
Horrid Henry. Dad said to write one
page. Henry would write one page. In
his biggest, most gigantic handwriting,
Henry wrote:

Dear Aunt Ruby,
Thank you
for the
Present.

Henry

That certainly filled a whole page, thought Horrid Henry.

Mom came into the room.

"Have you written your letters yet?"

"Yes," lied Henry.

Mom glanced over his shoulder.

"Henry!" said Mom. "That is not a proper thank you letter."

"Yes it is," snarled Henry. "Dad said to write one page so I wrote one page."

"Write five sentences," said Mom.

Five sentences? Five whole sentences? It was completely impossible for anyone to write so much. His hand would fall off.

"That's way too much," wailed Henry.

"No TV until you write your letters," said Mom, leaving the room.

Horrid Henry stuck out his tongue. He had the meanest, most horrible parents in the world. When he was king any parent who even whispered the words "thank you letter" would get fed to the crocodiles.

They wanted five sentences? He'd give them five sentences. Henry picked up his pencil and scrawled:

Dear Aunt Ruby,
No thank you for the horrible present. It is the worst present I have ever had.
Anyway, didn't some old Roman say it was better to give than to receive? So in fact, you should be writing me a thank you letter.
Henry
P.S. Next time just send money.

There! Five whole sentences. Perfect, thought Horrid Henry. Mom said he had to write a five sentence thank you letter. She never said it had to be a *nice* thank you letter. Suddenly Henry felt

quite cheerful. He folded the letter and
popped it in the stamped envelope Mom
had given him.

One down. Two to go.

In fact, Aunt Ruby's no thank you
letter would do just fine for Great-Aunt
Greta. He'd just substitute Great-Aunt
Greta's name for Aunt Ruby's and copy
the rest.

Bingo. Another letter was done.

Now, Grandma. She *had* sent money
so he'd have to write something nice.

"Thank you for the money, blah blah
blah, best present I've ever received, blah
blah blah, next year send more money,
$15 isn't very much, Ralph got $20 from
his grandma, blah blah blah."

What a waste, thought Horrid Henry
as he signed it and put it in the envelope,
to spend so much time on a letter, only
to have to write the same old thing all
over again next year.

And then suddenly Horrid Henry
had a wonderful, spectacular idea. Why
had he never thought of this before?
He would be rich, rich, rich. "There
goes money-bags Henry," kids would
whisper enviously, as he swaggered down
the street followed by Peter lugging a
hundred videos for Henry to watch in his
mansion on one of his twenty-eight giant
TVs. Mom and Dad and Peter would be
living in their hovel somewhere, and if
they were very, very nice to him Henry
might let them watch one of his smaller
TVs for fifteen minutes or so once a
month.

Henry was going to start a business. A business guaranteed to make him rich.

"Step right up, step right up," said Horrid Henry. He was wearing a sign saying: HENRY'S THANK YOU LETTERS. "Personal letters written just for you." A small crowd of children gathered round him.

"I'll write all your thank you letters for you," said Henry. "All you have to

do is to give me a stamped, addressed envelope and tell me what present you got. I'll do the rest."

"How much for a thank you letter?" asked Kung-Fu Kate.

"One dollar," said Henry.

"No way," said Greedy Graham.

"Ninety-nine cents," said Henry.

"Forget it," said Lazy Linda.

"OK, 50¢," said Henry. "And two for 75¢."

"Done," said Linda.

Henry opened his notebook. "And what were the presents?" he asked. Linda made a face. "Handkerchiefs," she spat. "And a bookmark."

"I can do a 'no thank you' letter," said Henry. "I'm very good at those."

Linda considered.

"Tempting," she said, "but then mean Uncle John won't send something better next time."

Business was booming. Dave bought
three. Ralph bought four "no thank
you's." Even Moody Margaret bought
one. Whoopee, thought Horrid Henry.
His pockets were jingle-jangling with
cash. Now all he had to do was to write
seventeen letters. Henry tried not to
think about that.

The moment he got home from school
Henry went straight to his room. Right,
to work, thought Henry. His heart sank
as he looked at the blank pages. All those
letters! He would be here for weeks.
Why had he ever set up a letter-writing
business?

But then Horrid Henry thought.
True, he'd promised a personal letter
but how would Linda's aunt ever find
out that Margaret's granny had received
the same one? She wouldn't! If he used
the computer, it would be a cinch. And
it would be a letter sent personally,

thought Henry, because I am a
person and I will personally print it
out and send it. All he'd have to do
was to write the names at the top and
to sign them. Easy-peasy lemon
squeezy.

Then again, all that signing. And
writing all those names at the top.
And separating the thank you letters
from the no thank you ones.

Maybe there was a better way.

Horrid Henry sat down at the
computer and typed:

Dear Sir or Madam,

That should cover everyone, thought
Henry, and I won't have to write
anyone's name.

Thank you /No thank you/ for the
a) wonderful

b) horrible

c) disgusting

present. I really loved it/hated it. In fact, it is the best present/worst present I have ever received. I played with it/ broke it/ ate it/ spent it/ threw it in the garbage right away. Next time just send lots of money.

Best wishes/ worst wishes

Now, how to sign it? Aha, thought Henry.

Your friend or relative.

Perfect, thought Horrid Henry. Sir or Madam knows whether they deserve a thank you or a no thank you letter. Let them do some work for a change and tick the correct answers.

Print.

Print.

Print.

Out spewed seventeen letters. It only took a moment to stuff them in the envelopes. He'd pop the letters in the mailbox on the way to school.

Had an easier way to become a millionaire ever been invented, thought Horrid Henry, as he turned on the TV?

Ding dong.

It was two weeks after Henry set up "Henry's Thank You Letters."

Horrid Henry opened the door.

A group of Henry's customers stood there, waving pieces of paper and shouting.

"My granny sent the letter back and now I can't watch TV for a week," wailed Moody Margaret.

"I'm grounded!" screamed Aerobic Al.

"I have to go swimming!" screamed Lazy Linda.

"No candy!" yelped Greedy Graham.

"No allowance!" screamed Rude Ralph.

"And it's all your fault!" they shouted.

Horrid Henry glared at his angry customers. He was outraged. After all his hard work, *this* was the thanks he got?

"Too bad!" said Horrid Henry as he slammed the door. Honestly, there was no pleasing some people.

"Henry," said Mom. "I just had the
strangest phone call from Aunt Ruby..."

Horrid Henry's
Family, Friends, and Enemies

Aerobic Al

Anxious Andrew

Aunt Ruby....................................

Beefy Bert....................

Bossy Bill...............................

Brainy Brian

Clever Clare......................

Dad...

Dizzy Dave.......................

Fiery Fiona

...............Fluffy the cat

Goody-Goody Gordon

Gorgeous Gurinder

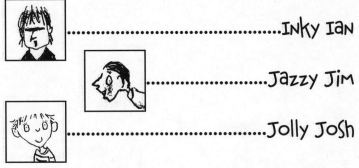................Grandpa

................Granny

Great Aunt Greta

Greedy Graham

................Inky Ian

................Jazzy Jim

................Jolly Josh

Jumpy Jeffrey

Kind Kasim

New Nick

Perfect Peter

Pimply Paul

Prissy Polly

Rabid Rebecca

Rude Ralph

Singing Saraya

Soggy Sid

Sour Susan

Stuck-up Steve

Tidy Ted

Tough Toby

Vain Violet......................................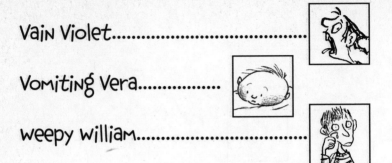

Vomiting Vera.................

weepy William.....................................

The HORRID HENRY books
by Francesca Simon

Illustrated by Tony Ross
Each book contains four stories

HORRID HENRY

Henry is dragged to dancing class against his will; vies with Moody Margaret to make the yuckiest Glop; goes camping; and tries to be good like Perfect Peter—but not for long.

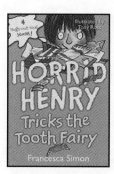

HORRID HENRY TRICKS THE TOOTH FAIRY

Horrid Henry tries to trick the Tooth Fairy into giving him more money; sends Moody Margaret packing; causes his teachers to run screaming from school; and single-handedly wrecks a wedding.

HORRID HENRY and THE MEGA-MEAN TIME MACHINE

Horrid Henry reluctantly goes for a hike; builds a time machine and convinces Perfect Peter that boys wear dresses in the future; Perfect Peter plays one of the worst tricks ever on his brother; and Henry's aunt takes the family to a fancy restaurant, so his parents bribe him to behave.

HORRID HENRY'S STINKBOMB

Horrid Henry uses a stinkbomb as a toxic weapon in his long-running war with Moody Margaret; uses all his tricks to win the school reading competition; goes for a sleepover and retreats in horror when he finds that other people's houses aren't always as nice as his own; and has the joy of seeing Miss Battle-Axe in hot water with the principal when he knows it was all his fault.

HORRID HENRY
AND THE
MUMMY'S CURSE

Horrid Henry indulges his favorite hobby— collecting Gizmos; has a bad time with his spelling homework; starts a rumor that there's a shark in the pool; and spooks Perfect Peter with the mummy's curse.

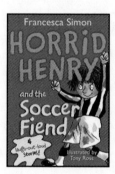

HORRID HENRY
AND THE
SOCCER FIEND

Horrid Henry reads
Perfect Peter's diary and
improves it; goes shopping
with Mom and tries to make her buy
him some really nice new sneakers; is
horrified when his old enemy Bossy
Bill turns up at school; and tries by any
means, to win the class soccer match.

HORRID HENRY
AND THE
SCARY SITTER

Horrid Henry encounters
the worst babysitter in
the world; traumatizes
his parents on a long car trip; is banned
from trick-or-treating at Halloween;
and emerges victorious from a raid on
Moody Margaret's Secret Club.

HORRiD HENRY'S CHRISTMAS

Horrid Henry sabotages the Christmas play; tries to do all his Christmas shopping without spending any of his allowance; attempts to ambush Santa Claus (to get more presents of course); and has to endure the worst Christmas dinner ever!

About the Author

Photo: Francesco Guidicini

Francesca Simon spent her childhood on the beach in California and then went to Yale and Oxford Universities to study medieval history and literature. She now lives in London with her family. She has written over forty-five books and won the Children's Book of the Year in 2008 at the Galaxy British Book Awards for *Horrid Henry and the Abominable Snowman*.